THE QUEEN

OF

SERPENTS

Alexander Bischoff

Alexander Bischoff

Table of Contents

Alexander Bischoff

I want to express my heartfelt gratitude to my incredible mother and my dear friends Calvin, George, and Aimee, including my Douglas, for their unwavering support and creative input. Without them, this story would not have evolved into what it is today, and I am immensely grateful for that. Their love and encouragement have been invaluable throughout this journey.

Crafting this story has been a labor of love, and it brings me immense joy to share it with you. I poured my heart and soul into its creation, hoping to touch the hearts of all those who read it. I sincerely wish that you experience the same joy and delight I felt while weaving this tale.

Chapter

One

The modest house in Athens, nestled in a tranquil corner of the village, stands unassuming, crafted from stone and clay, with a thatched roof and a small garden gracing the front.

Inside, Medusa lays in bed, slowly lifting her head and fixing her gaze upon her father. Her mother passed away during childbirth, but her father has always been there to care for her. Kneeling beside her, he kisses her on the forehead, preparing to tell one of her favorite stories.

"Once upon a time, in the ancient city of Hellas, a great rivalry exists between two powerful gods, Athena and Poseidon. Athena, the goddess of wisdom and strategy, and Poseidon, the god of the sea, desire to be this magnificent city's patron deity.

The people of Athens are puzzled over whom they should choose as their protector. Seeking the wisdom of the Oracle at Delphi, they are told to hold a contest between the two gods. Each god will present a gift to the city, and the people will decide which blessing has more significant value.

On the chosen day, the citizens of Athens gather in the heart of their city - a grand courtyard where the gods would showcase their offerings. Anticipation fills the air as Poseidon steps forward first. With a mighty wave of his trident, he strikes the earth, causing a beautiful spring of salt water to erupt, transforming it into a magnificent fountain. The people marvel at the sight, grateful for Poseidon's generous gift. However, they know that salty water is unsuitable for their crops and cannot sustain them.

Then, it is Athena's turn to present her gift. Gracefully and confidently, she plants a single seed into the earth. The people watch in awe as a lush and magnificent olive tree sprouts from the ground. Its branches reach high into the sky, providing shade, and its fruit is a bountiful source of food and oil. The citizens are overjoyed by the practicality and abundance of Athena's gift.

The people of Hellas recognize the value of Athena's contribution and declare her the contest winner. They acknowledge her as the patron goddess of their city by changing the name to Athens, as she has bestowed upon them a gift that will sustain them for generations to come.

Poseidon understands and respects Athena's decision, even though he feels ashamed of his loss. He vows to maintain a harmonious relationship with her.

And so, Athens flourished under the watchful guidance of Athena, the goddess of wisdom. The olive tree becomes a symbol of the city's prosperity and knowledge, while Poseidon's fountain serves as a reminder of his defeat.

From that day forward, the people of Athens cherish the legacy of the contest between Athena and Poseidon, always remembering the wisdom of their chosen patron goddess.

"Do you think Poseidon resents Athena for being defeated?" Medusa asks her father.

"Perhaps, but we shall never know. Like us, the gods must learn from their mistakes to grow. Perhaps they are so much so that they have left petty revenge and greed behind."

"But isn't greed what started it?" Medusa questioned thoughtfully.

"It did indeed," he smiles at his daughter. "Now, go to sleep. We have a big day ahead of us tomorrow." He kisses Medusa on the forehead and blows out the candle.

Chapter

Two

The following year, tragedy strikes as Medusa's father chokes on an olive and tragically passes away during dinner. Medusa feels powerless as she watches her father fade away, and she runs to get help, but it is too late. In the following days, Medusa isolates herself, spending her time alone until a sudden knock on the door makes her fall silent. As she swings open the door, a beautiful woman appears, her silk floor-length veil glowing in the moonlight.

"Hello, my name is Amaltea," the woman introduces herself. "Are you Medusa?"

Medusa weakly nods in response. Amaltea recognizes the shock that has taken hold of Medusa but knows she must act swiftly. She guides Medusa into a nearby room and assists her in settling into a chair, offering a comforting presence.

"Let me attend to you," Amaltea's voice resonates gently, brimming with empathy. She runs her fingers through Medusa's vibrant dark emerald hair with delicate strokes, soothingly brushing away the tangled strands. As she assists Medusa in removing her worn garments, Amaltea carefully lays out fresh clothes, a tangible gesture of care and compassion.

With a voice that blends sympathy and fortitude, Amaltea says, comforting Medusa's wounded soul, "Fear not, Medusa. Your Father now flows freely beside your mother in the river of eternity. Though you bear the weight of their absence, I'm here to offer support and a new beginning."

Tears well up in Medusa's eyes, reflecting the depths of her sorrow, as she slowly nods, acknowledging Amaltea's comforting presence. She begins to realize that she doesn't have to face this difficult journey alone. Amaltea stands as an unwavering pillar of solace and support in this pivotal moment of vulnerability, embracing Medusa with steadfast love and understanding.

Chapter

Three

Elder Priestess Amaltea meticulously trained the young priestesses of Crete, subjecting them to rigorous education in literature, philosophy, and strategy. At the same time, they devoted themselves to the sacred vows of the temple. As Athena sees the new group of orphaned girls arriving on the island, bereft of parents, her heart brims with empathy and sorrow from her celestial orb.

Walking through the grand halls of the temple's library, Athena keenly sees the new initiates, her admiration growing with each passing moment. Elder Priestess Amaltea calls out the names of the newcomers, presenting Medusa with her first textbook and extending a warm welcome to the priesthood. Athena's gaze lingers on Medusa's stunning beauty, pausing from her duties of organizing books, particularly her long dark emerald hair, as she follows Amaltea to her assigned quarters.

Entering her new room, Medusa is greeted with warmth by Melia. "Hello, I'm Melia," she cheerfully introduces herself. Medusa reciprocates with a warm smile, replying, "I'm Medusa. Nice to meet you." Melia loves Medusa's distinctive dark emerald hair, and she can't help but compliment it. "Wow, your hair is amazing! I love how it gleams in the light," she expresses with an authentic smile.

A sensation stirs within Medusa's chest, but this time it is one of positivity. Melia's kind words carry profound significance for her, having faced ridicule because of her hair. "Thank you so much," Medusa responds, her smile growing wider. "It's truly refreshing to meet someone who appreciates it finally."

In that simple exchange and Melia's genuine compliment, Medusa experiences a surge of hope and a profound sense of belonging. She has stumbled upon the opportunity to embark on a new chapter in her life where she can be her true self.

Chapter

Four

The grand and ancient structure of the temple stood on the hill, paying homage to the mighty goddess Athena. Gleaming marble comprised its form, with intricate carvings adorning the columns at the entrance, portraying vivid scenes of Athena blessing Athens and Hercules. As the priestesses ascended the marble steps leading up to the temple, Medusa and Melia conversed quietly, trailing behind. Athena kept a watchful eye on them, finding pleasure in observing their prayers. However, today, Melia and Medusa whispered to each other during the service, resembling mischievous students in a tedious class.

Elder Sophia, standing at the forefront of the priestess group in her veil, commands attention as she addresses them. "Let us unite in silence and pay homage to Athena through our sacred vows," she declares.

The girls fall silent, respectfully bowing their heads as Elder Sophia initiates the recitation of the vows. They articulate their commitments in unison:

"I will never use Athena's name in vain."

"I will abstain from marriage."

"I will uphold the honor of this temple."

"I will offer prayers solely to Athena."

"To Athena, we pledge unwavering loyalty."

Completing the recitation of their vows, the priestesses lifted their heads, their gazes expectant, as if seeking validation for their unwavering devotion to Athena. They believed it was their duty to remain loyal to the goddess, regardless of whether she deserved it. Medusa grasped the principle, even if she didn't entirely agree. To her, it seemed unjust that the fleeting happiness of a deity should take precedence over her own.

Chapter

Five

T en years passed, and the temple gathered knowledge, shaping the lives of its devoted priestesses. Unfortunately, that knowledge didn't prevent the fires that decimated their island and crops. As the years went by, Medusa learnt not to question the actions of the gods.

Instead, she directed her attention to advanced philosophy. Elder Sophia had previously introduced them to the works of Thales of Miletus, which attempted to explain the laws of the universe and the soul. However, Amaltea recently received a new scripture and felt enlightened by it.

With the sun illuminating her face through the carved-out windows, Amaltea began the class. The girls sat on the floor around her as she said, "Recently, a man named Zeno has offered a fresh perspective on the human experience. He suggests focusing all your energy solely on things within one's control and diminishing attention to others' actions towards you. Instead, he stressed the importance of reflecting on past actions and considering future steps for resolution. Zeno also spoke about gauging success by the effort exerted rather than by tallying achievements."

Phaedra scoffed, stating, "Sounds like he lost his mind."

But, Amaltea promptly retorted, "I think it's actually quite profound, my dear."

"I agree," added Medusa, her voice unwavering.

Later that evening, after their class, Medusa and Melia found themselves engaged in an intense game of spitting olive seeds into a ring of stones, savoring their last moments of freedom in the open field. Although Melia disliked olives like Medusa, she lacked her friend's precision in spitting them. From the celestial orb in the temple, Athena watched them with a mix of interest and contentment.

Suddenly, Phaedra, accompanied by Chryseis and Nephele, interrupted their game, approaching with a malicious sneer. She condescended to them, labeling them as "outcasts."

With caution, Melia asked for Phaedra's intentions, saying, "What do you want?"

"I wanted to invite you to play a game with us. It'll be better with more people," Phaedra says, grabbing Medusa's arm and pulling her towards them. Medusa remains unimpressed and resolute, rejecting the offer. "No, thank you. We're fine on our own," she retorts.

"Suit yourself. You do seem to enjoy your privacy," Phaedra replies, her tone now slightly offended.

"Fine, we'll play your stupid game," Melia snaps.

Approaching their group of friends, Phaedra confidently declares, "I told you they'd agree," earning smiles from the other girls. "Let's play a game where we take turns expressing what we appreciate about the person to our right," she suggests.

As the game progresses with ordinary compliments, tension rises. When it's Phaedra's turn, she delivers a hurtful bombshell, saying, "I appreciate Medusa's ability to brown nose her way into being Amaltea's favorite. If I were that fake, I'm sure she'd like me too." The group gasps and laughs at the insult.

But Medusa, not one to be silenced, retaliates with a subtle jab, "I appreciate that Melia tries to find redeeming qualities about Phaedra when there are clearly none." The girls giggle again, clearly amused.

Melia follows suit, "I appreciate Medusa's beauty, which surpasses even that of Phaedra, and her hair is more unique than Athena's." But then the girls fall silent.

The comparison to Athena prompts a reaction from the group. Phaedra retorts, mocking Melia's affection, "Melia, your affection for Medusa must blind you because all I see is a head of grass." Laughter breaks out among the girls once again.

Amaltea intervenes and inquires, "Girls, what's going on?"

Phaedra accuses Melia, "Melia used Athena's name in vain."

Amaltea examines the girls deeply and asks for their side of the story.

Chryseis and Nephele quickly nod in agreement.

Medusa remains silent, not wanting to worsen the situation for Melia or herself.

Amaltea feels disappointed and turns to Melia, saying, "I thought I taught you better. We are going to have to have a chat with Elder Sophia." She firmly takes hold of Melia's arm and pulls her away.

Medusa desperately wants to explain and defend her friend, but fear holds her back.

Meanwhile, Athena witnesses the whole scene with disapproval before turning away from her orb, troubled by what she sees."

***

That night, Medusa ate a small portion of smashed olives and sipped a tiny cup of goat milk for dinner. She sat with her friends, but Melia's spot remained empty. As she looked at her food, her distaste for olives and reminders of her father's passing took over, so she savored her quarter glass of milk. Before each meal, they thanked Athena for their 'plentiful' food, even though everyone had grown tired of olives. However, looking at her plate, Medusa didn't think 'plentiful' was the right word.

The recent bushfires on the island had decimated their usual diet of fabulous greek salad. The flames had consumed all other crops, leaving them with only olives.

Only the crops in the elevated landscapes above sea level had survived.

At last, Melia returned, informing her, "Elder Sophia wants to see you in the goat pen. I just relayed what transpired."

Medusa responded, "That sounds best," before heading to the enclosure. There, she saw Elder Priestess Sophia milking a goat in the sunset's glow, determinedly extracting every drop.

Medusa said, "You requested me sister."

"Yes, Medusa. I always thought you to be loyal," Elder Sophia replied and looked into Medusa's eyes.

"I try to be."

"Then why did you not stand by your Melia?"

"I was scared it would only confirm Phaedra's story."

"Never be scared of the truth. It is a powerful thing."

"I agree. I will stop allowing that to weaken me."

"Good, and never let fear control you either. You must always follow your heart."

"Deal."

"Good. Now, off to bed."

Chapter

Six

Medusa lay in bed, unsatisfied with the supper and lost in thought about her conversation with Elder Sophia. Her belly griped for more food, and she couldn't find rest, tossing and turning. Eventually, she got up and asked Melia, "Do you want to go for a walk?"

"Yes," Melia replied with a smile, swinging off her olive wood bed frame. Together, they slipped out of the sleeping quarters and strolled along the shoreline, illuminated solely by moonlight.

"Melia, I'm sorry about earlier," said Medusa. "It made me nervous, and I didn't know what to say."

"It's ok, I understand," replied Melia. "Everyone knows Phaedra is just a bully."

"Ugh, Phaedra is such a pain, and I swear she won't give us a break," Medusa grumbled.

Melia nodded in agreement, sharing the same sentiment. "She's absolutely the worst."

Medusa sighed, wishing for a world where Phaedra would disappear. "I wish I could just erase her from my life."

Melia empathized, understanding the impossibility of such a wish. "I feel you, but we can't waste our energy on impossible dreams."

Medusa proposed a new idea. "You know what? Let's think about leaving Crete," she suggested, steering the conversation toward a fresh perspective.

"Leave Crete? Come on, Phaedra isn't that bad," Melia retorted. "Besides, she usually only belittles me. It will pass."

"Yes, but perhaps I have more reasons," Medusa said. "You see, I want to explore the world. I'm tired of eating endless olives and worshiping a goddess who doesn't help." Moonlight highlights Medusa's cheekbones.

"Would you really abandon your priesthood?" Melia, backlit by the moon and crashing waves, asked.

"I mean, we would embark on a journey for a while. I want to see what else exists out there," Medusa clarified.

"But Sophia would never allow us to return if we did," Melia reminded with a hint of worry.

"What if she made an exception for us?" Medusa proposed, her eyes filled with hope.

"You made a solemn oath never to leave. What meaning do our vows hold if you break them? It would be a betrayal of Athena," Melia expressed, her tone tinged with concern.

"You just spoke her name in vain! Athena has never shown us any honour. So why should we concern ourselves with honouring her?" Medusa argued, frustration evident in her voice.

Melia said, "Well, I regret uttering those words, and I care. I don't want to disappoint Amaltea and Sophia, and I have no interest in riling the gods." She turned away from Medusa, her face displaying a mix of emotions.

"Fine. I'll go alone then," Medusa declared

"Do you intend to leave me?" Melia asked, her voice filled with hurt and confusion.

"I don't see any reason not to," Medusa retorted, her voice tinged with disappointment. "I was trying to help you. But if you choose not to come, you'll have to endure Phaedra's torment."

Melia took a deep breath, attempting to contain her frustration. "Fine. If you enjoy being alone, enjoy your solitary stroll." With that, she turned around and stormed back, leaving Medusa alone on the beach, engulfed in solitude.

Medusa felt the urge to raise her hands towards the sky, but a different inspiration struck her. Fuelled by this idea, she marched up the hill determinedly towards Athena's temple, and with a sense of reverence, she knelt on both knees just before the prayer commenced, ensuring she performed the act with utmost sincerity. It was time to take matters into her own hands.

"Please Poseidon, I call upon you," she whispers with desperation in her voice. "My priesthood starves, and our goddess has failed us."

"Your voice is beautiful," says the handsome older man. Medusa turns to see him standing at the temple's entrance, wearing only a rather small swimming robe.

Surprise shows on Medusa's face as she inquires, "Thank you, how do you know my name?" She feels perplexed by his sudden appearance and attire.

A chuckle escapes the man's lips. "I have come to claim you as my wife, Medusa," he declares, his tone dripping with arrogance.

Medusa's eyes widen, revealing a hint of panic. "I'm sorry, but I cannot accept. I am a devoted priestess."

"I already own the right to you," he says, producing a contract listing Medusa's name under 'property' and Poseidon's under 'owner'.

Medusa meets the old man's gaze, a wave of recognition dawning on her as she discerns his true identity. "My people starve, Poseidon. Please help feed them, and I will marry you."

"I will hear none of this," the man instantly transforms, donning a gold plated body armour adorned with a coral crown and wielding a majestic golden trident. He grabs Medusa, pinning her against the wall.

"I had hoped you would come to your senses, but it's disheartening that you required the revelation of my true power to convince you," Poseidon remarks.

"I am truly sorry, Poseidon." Medusa implores, genuine remorse in her voice.

A menacing promise escapes Poseidon's lips as he declares, "For your defiance, I shall punish you." With a swift motion, he strikes Medusa in the ribs with his golden trident. Overwhelmed with horror, Medusa collapses to the floor, her body consumed by pain.

"I will have you as my wife, and there shall be no negotiations," Poseidon declares, his tone resolute.

Poseidon raises the trident high, summoning the full force of his mighty waves, crashing through the temple and pulling Medusa toward the depths of his ocean. The tumultuous waters engulf her, and her desperate arms flail, unable to breathe as she sinks into the abyss.

However, the connection between Poseidon and the wave suddenly shatters, a brilliant light striking the scene, causing both the wave and Poseidon to vanish instantly.

Medusa cries out upon seeing Athena behind the storm. "Athena! You have come to help me?" But Athena is not there to show mercy.

"I can't believe you'd do this!" Athena's voice booms in anger. "I truly apologize," Medusa says desperately. "Your people starve." The sand beneath medusa's fingers began to move.

"You've brought shame upon me," Athena declares sharply. "If you truly regretted it, you wouldn't have done it." A massive dark green serpent bursts from the sand.

Medusa pleads again, desperation in her voice. "Please, we desperately need food." She meets the glowing red eyes of the now eight foot tall creature.

"If you forsake my loyalty, then fear me instead," Athena warns with dark intent.

Medusa senses the goddess's intense fury, aware she's caused it.

In a voice dripping with anger, Athena declares, "From today, no mortal shall look upon your hair until death do them part." The serpent lunges toward Medusa and bites her neck, and her vision fades too black.

THE QUEEN OF SERPENTS

Chapter

Seven

After encountering Medusa, Athena returns to her temple in the dark, staring into her orb as if she believes it will guide her. But it is only showing her Medusa's unconscious legs on the beach. She waits for her to wake up, but the vision within her orb shifts.

Now, it shows her Poseidon walking up toward the capital.

He looks as magnificent in person as she remembers, tall with silver hair shining like an ocean as it flows behind him! How can any male have such beautiful hair?

Nevertheless, as glorious as he looks, Athena feels suspicious of his intent with each step he takes toward Athens. She wonders what he's up to. He goes to the glass fountain and chants, the sounds putting an ancient curse on it. The water before him turns murky, beginning to flow down Athens 'streets thickly like blood!

Athena walks away from her orb with a furrowed brow, blindly fuming over Poseidon's curse and wanting nothing more but to lash out at something or someone until she feels a bit better.

***

Athena watches Medusa, as she sleeps. The sound of a familiar voice finally awakens her.

"Medusa? Medusa?" calls Melia. Medusa opens her eyes and gets up, but when the two girls 'eyes meet, there is a pause in which neither moves. It seems time has stopped for both of them as they stare at each other.

Confused by Melia's stillness, Medusa gets up and runs toward her. Athena sees that Melia's skin is no longer flesh but stone. Medusa tries to run for help, but her legs are weak, and she quickly stumbles. Catching her foot on a root, Medusa tumbles down the rest of the hill, smashing her knee against a rock. Miraculously, she gets back up and runs for someone to assist her. Then she sees a piece of her new hair and screams, throwing it off her face, terrified to touch her head.

Medusa hears Elder Sophia calling her name. She responds, "Go away, please," but Elder Sophia runs to her voice, finding her behind the teaching hall. Medusa looks up to see Elder Sophia frozen in lifeless stone.

The sun has only just risen, but already the heat is oppressive. Medusa feels beads of sweat trickling down her back, leaving a trail of goosebumps behind. It pools in the small of her back, prickly, uncomfortable, and deeply unpleasant. She has only gone a few yards when she hears another familiar voice yell and sees someone run away, screaming, "Beast!"

She turns and sees Phaedra sitting in the washroom with a pale and terrified face. Medusa feels a surge of dread as she looks at her, but Phaedra turns to stone before she can react. Medusa feels hot and nauseous, needing to splash water on her face. She hurtles toward the well and then sees her reflection, trying not to faint.

She gets back up and once again looks at herself, then quickly turns away.

Athena realizes that she has transformed Medusa's once beautiful hair into living serpents and that she may have been partly responsible for the death of Melia, Elder Sophia, and Phaedra. She senses Medusa's guilt and sickness. Attempting to get up, Medusa sees her entire priesthood has gathered in the field. She tries to hide, but it is too late. Each Priestess screams, making the others look around and meet the serpent's eyes.

The power of their new gaze is undeniable, and the consequences are inescapable. The thought of running crosses Medusa's mind, yet her feet seem firmly planted, rendering any attempt futile.

As Medusa collapses, her gaze falls upon her entire priesthood, each now frozen in a state of anguish and terror, transformed into stone by the chilling sight of her. Their petrified forms lie before her, a testament to the havoc she has wrought.

Amaltea is the only one facing the other direction and the last to witness her. The frozen disappointment etched on Amaltea's face haunts Medusa's thoughts, an indelible image she cannot erase.

Burdened by remorse, Athena recognizes the consequences of her actions and feels her heart ache with regret. Yet, she can only stand as a helpless spectator, observing the transformed Medusa, now a being both feared and despised. At that moment, her serpents begin to hiss, amplifying the tension in the air.

Powerlessness and entrapment engulf Medusa in that pivotal moment as she witnesses the devastating reality unfolding before her. Instead of offering solace, her serpents torment her with incessant hisses, placing the blame squarely on her shoulders. Their venomous voices echo, proclaiming, "It's all your fault."

Summoning every ounce of strength within her, Medusa rises to her feet, propelled forward by an urgent desire for refuge, a place she can turn to — Athena's temple. Each step she takes quickens the pace of her pounding heart, urging her to seek forgiveness and atone for the irreparable damage she has caused.

Finally reaching the temple, she collapses to her knees, overwhelmed by her emotions as she pours out prayers and pleas for absolution. The serpents 'relentless chant of accusations makes it impossible to concentrate, yet Medusa persists, vowing to do whatever is necessary to set things right. She yearns for a sign, a glimmer of response from the goddess she once revered, but all she receives is the persistent hissing of her serpents. With each passing moment, their sounds serve as a bitter reminder of her betrayal, and it becomes increasingly evident that Athena will not bestow forgiveness upon her.

Despite the relentless hissing, Medusa remains there, kneeling at the feet of the statue, long into the night, desperately clinging to hope, praying for a shift in her fortunes. However, as the sun begins its ascent on the horizon, she is compelled to accept the agonizing truth that Athena has abandoned her in her hour of need. The weight of this realization crashes down upon her, leaving her feeling forsaken and utterly alone.

Chapter

Eight

In a display of spite, Poseidon disguised himself as a wealthy fisherman and visited the palace in Athens. He offered the King a magnificent golden chariot filled with fish, pulled by horses, as a gift. The King enthusiastically welcomed the fisherman and was thrilled with the generous offering.

Poseidon warned the King about a great danger, saying, "My Lord, I have come to inform you that a Gorgon has been created on the island of Crete. It is capable of leaving the island even at this moment."

Upon hearing this, the King's face grew dark, and he demanded further information. He summoned his sons Xabthos, Perseus, and Pythios to the throne room. There, they found the King seated on his ornate throne, wearing a smile. As they entered, Xabthos and Pythios came to attention and stopped. However, Perseus, the rightful heir to the throne, stepped forward with curiosity.

When the King saw Perseus, his expression faltered, and he avoided eye contact, clearly regarding Perseus as nothing more than a reminder of his late wife. Nevertheless, Perseus was determined to change his father's perception of him and earn the respect and recognition he deserved as the true heir.

Although Perseus was the sole descendant of the former King, he had always felt like an outsider in his kingdom. He had tirelessly worked to prove himself, but his efforts were often met with disparagement. Now, standing in the presence of the King, Perseus finally had an opportunity to demonstrate his worth. He was resolved not to let this chance slip away.

The King, a tall man with piercing eyes and a stern demeanor, addressed the gathering in a subdued voice. "Today, I have summoned you for a grave matter—a troubling piece of news. It is the greatest threat our kingdom has ever faced. A Gorgon has been born, and if it reaches Athens, we will all perish under its everlasting gaze. A fisherman reports that our priestesses in Crete have all but disappeared. The Gorgon possesses serpentine qualities and the power to turn people to stone with its gaze. I am eager to hear your insights on this dire situation."

Perseus, his initial bravado wavering as he grasped the magnitude of the mission, asked tentatively, "How can we possibly confront such a formidable foe?" Inwardly, he winced, aware of the constant insults and snide remarks hurled at him by his stepbrothers.

However, it was too late; the King absorbed his words and crafted a composed response. "Thankfully, the fisherman has provided me with three highly reflective shields. In addition, rely on your seafaring skills, sharpened instincts, and trusty blade. Though you may not share my bloodline, with your brothers by your side, I have unwavering faith that you can conquer any dragon or menacing sea creature that crosses your path."

Pythios, Perseus 'brother, scornfully spat, "Ha! As if Perseus will be the one to vanquish the beast! Unless he expects to be able to read it a bedtime story. He is likelier to flee from it, wailing like a maiden."

Disregarding the taunt, Perseus and the King remained unfazed. Yet, standing nearby, Xabthos, the second brother, wore a mocking grin, struggling to suppress a laugh that eventually burst forth, filling the room with mirth.

Undeterred by the tension, the King announced with conviction, "Your ships await you, ready for departure. Each of you must embark on this perilous quest alone. The one who returns bearing the head of this colossal creature shall be declared my rightful successor."

Perseus understood the King's underlying motive—his belief that his lesser-regarded brothers, Pythios or Xabthos, stood a greater chance of triumph in a ruthless battle.

Chapter

Nine

Gaia, the highly respected Greek goddess of the earth, tends to her garden and gazes into her crystal orb, where she sees Medusa praying to her in desperate need of help. Gaia, being the benevolent deity she is, understands the gravity of the situation and sets out on a journey to visit a cherished friend who can help her provide the aid that Medusa requires.

Arachne, a minuscule spider no larger than a coin, possessed a rounded body and eight delicate legs. Her beady black eyes, round and shining with intelligence, captivated attention. Arachne's origins could be traced back to her skill as a talented weaver who dared to proclaim her superiority over Athena. This proclamation filled Athena with fury, prompting her to propose a weaving competition to Arachne promptly. Unfortunately for Athena, Arachne's creativity proved to be as magnificent as she had claimed, swiftly exposing Athena's shortcomings in the presence of the gods.

Driven mad by this, Athena cursed Arachne and turned her into a spider. Gaia briefly regards the spider, then says, "I need your help."

Arachne gazes upon the goddess and asks, "To make you another bedspread?"

"No."

"Curtains?"

"No."

"A coverlet?"

"No, I would appreciate your listening to my request. Athena has cursed a girl, and I need your help to protect her."

"Oh, then our not-so-favorite witch is at it again. In that case, how can I be of service?"

"Her newest victim desperately needs new clothing to cover her new hair."

"Oh, I see."

"Furthermore," Gaia adds, "It is crucial to inform her that Hades can solely nullify the curse before the Lunar Eclipse. However, she needs to acquire the pomegranate of the underworld beforehand and present it to him."

Arachne recoils. "How in the underworld am I, a spider, supposed to help her do all that? Also, why didn't anyone offer this to me?"

Gaia replies, "Time is of the essence. It would be best if you go now. Three princes are already on their way to kill her."

With a snap of her fingers, Arachne reappears in front of Medusa, who is praying for a way out of her curse.

***

Medusa lay on the frigid stone floor, consumed by inconsolable sobs, her desperate pleas for forgiveness echoing with each repetition of Athena's name. Suddenly, breaking the deafening silence, Arachne's voice pierced through.

"It's futile to seek Athena's aid," Arachne declared. "Gods cannot undo their curses upon mortals. I used to believe other gods couldn't either, until recently."

"Who's there? Reveal yourself!" demanded Medusa, her searching gaze scanning the surroundings for the source of the voice.

"It's me, Arachne—the spider," the voice responded. "I, too, have been cursed by Athena, but I can help you." Arachne began weaving intricate circles around Medusa. "Gods have no control over how their curses unfold. They always obtain what they desire, but there's always an unexpected price to pay. The strength of their emotions determines the potency of the curse."

"Arachne," Medusa whispered, brimming with curiosity. "How did you find me?"

Arachne smirked, mischief gleaming in her eyes amid the dimness. "Gaia sent me," she whispered inaudibly. "She believes that if you can locate the pomegranate of the underworld and present it to Hades before the lunar Eclipse, he might be able to break your curse."

Medusa's eyes widened as her gaze fell upon the emerald green veil and robe skillfully crafted by Arachne, matching her piercing eyes. "Is this true?" she asked, her astonishment evident.

Arachne nodded. "To my knowledge, you were destined to endure life as a beast like me, but yes, that's what Gaia conveyed."

Overflowing with gratitude, Medusa trembled as she admired the exquisite garments. "I'm willing to do whatever it takes to break this curse," she declared, her voice brimming with determination.

Yet, a harsh reality swiftly overshadowed her momentary elation. The veil could suppress her lethal abilities, but any rebellion from her serpentine locks risked unraveling the protective enchantment, leaving her vulnerable to the curse's dire consequences. The underworld's policy forbidding return visits further compounded her troubles. Just when it seemed that circumstances couldn't grow more dire, word reached Medusa of three princes en route to assassinate her.

As the weight of her impending fate pressed upon her, a sarcastic remark escaped Medusa's lips.

"Oh, wonderful!

Just what I needed—more complications.

Any ideas, Arachne?"

In response, her serpents hissed, "Doomed to die." Rolling her eyes, Medusa retorted, "Quiet!" She struck her veil, momentarily silencing the serpents 'voices.

Chapter

Ten

As Perseus set out on his journey to Crete, he knew he was likely to face a confrontation with his brothers Pythios and Xabthos. When he arrived at his boat, he discovered the sail had been torn. Luckily, Perseus had been laboring on a new sail. The new material he had chosen was lighter and capable of exerting a greater pull. He replaced the torn sail and resolutely set off to reach Crete before his brothers.

Thanks to his quick thinking and superior sailing knowledge, he successfully docks his boat on the island well ahead of them. While searching the island, the sight of the petrified girls deeply saddens Perseus. He uses his shield to look around corners, but there is no sign of the serpent. He feels the weight of responsibility to uncover the truth and seek justice for them. He goes to the temple at the top of the hill, where he sees Medusa in the reflection of his shield.

Fear and anticipation ripple through Medusa, mingling with a heady excitement as she meets the reflection of the man's gaze. He stands with commanding stature, every curve and edge of his physique hinting at strength, his sword and shield ready. Undaunted by her, his magnetic aura of confidence pulls her in. "You have nothing to fear," he asserts, voice dripping with allure.

"Go away" she yells aloud, her voice betraying a hint of intrigue.

"I've come to slay the serpent plaguing your people."

She can feel the heat of his presence intensifying her heartbeat. "Well, that is promising news." Her serpents hiss protectively, "Beware." But she silences them, noting that he seems unaware of their whispered warnings and seems more intent on discerning the true source of danger. Her heart flutters when she realizes he doesn't see her as the monster, and her usual stoic gaze softens. A playful smirk plays on her lips. "Your bravery is... captivating."

His brow furrows with genuine concern, "Are you all right? Were you one of the priestesses?" Pushing down her rising desire, Medusa tilts her head slightly, "A little shaken, but unscathed. Yes, I was one of the priestesses, caught up in prayer when the chaos began."

The electric charge between them is palpable, the weight of unsaid words and suppressed desires pressing on them.

"I'm sorry if I startled you," he murmurs, his eyes lingering on hers, stepping closer, bridging the gap.

"It's quite all right," she responds, her voice quivering slightly as the distance between them diminishes.

His voice drops, sultry and serious, "Have you seen the serpent? I'm here to defeat it, in competition with my brothers. Help me find it, and together, we could save many."

His gaze captures her, and she hesitates, searching for words, before offering, "It was a massive dark green serpent. I last saw it heading back out to sea." Internally, she weaves a delicate web of deception to protect her secret.

"Out to sea? Into the ocean?" Perseus asks, surprise evident on his face. "I never knew serpents could swim."

"Yes," she replies, standing by her fabricated tale. "It's a sea serpent, I believe. The work of the sea god."

"I see," Perseus acknowledged, a tinge of disappointment in his voice. "It seems that he no longer favors our people."

Perseus noticed Medusa's hesitation as he prepared to depart from the temple. Curiosity sparked within him, urging him to observe her more closely.

Medusa attempted to reassure Perseus of her well-being, but he remained steadfast in his belief that it was unwise for her to stay alone. Gradually, he convinced her to accompany him, assuring her of her safety under his watch. Medusa worried that this was all just a trap.

Medusa glanced at Arachne's attire, recognizing its effectiveness, and wondered if she could adapt to her curse. However, she knew that her immediate priority was to leave Crete, locate the pomegranate, find Hades, and end everything before the Lunar Eclipse.

***

Perseus descended the sandy hill, his footsteps raising dust in their wake. "How long have you lived here?" he asked, trying to start a conversation.

"Since I was fiver," replied Medusa, her voice soft and tinged with nostalgia.

Perseus surveyed the idyllic landscape of Crete. "This place is breathtaking. I wish I had grown up here instead of in Athens," he confessed, bitterness seeping into his tone.

"Really? Sometimes, I miss Athens' energy," Medusa admitted, a hint of longing in her voice.

Perseus sighed. "Ah, Athens. It's a beautiful city, but it faces its share of challenges. Starvation and illness plague the people. I wish I knew how to help, but my father believes we're already doing too much."

Medusa nodded thoughtfully. "I believe that wise investment in Greece can create new wealth for everyone."

"Wow, I've never heard someone articulate what I believe so perfectly."

"I'm glad," they both fell silent, looking into each other's eyes.

To break the silence, Medusa spoke again, "I've always wished I could have grown up in Athens with my parents. It seems so sophisticated and exhilarating."

"It's funny how we often desire what we don't have. It's like a curse," Perseus remarked, a small smile playing on his lips.

Arachne rolled her eyes, unable to contain her sarcasm. "Wow, so profound," she commented.

THE QUEEN OF SERPENTS

Perseus turned to her, sensing the tension in the air. "Did you say something?"

"No," Medusa swiftly denied, her intuition guiding her response.

"Oh, my mistake. I thought I heard something," Perseus said, continuing his descent down the hill toward the schoolhouse.

Then Perseus pointed to the two men standing by the statues. "Those must be my idiot brothers."

Once in earshot, Pythios yelled, "Who is this pretty thing you've brought us, Perseus?"

Perseus says, "Her name is Medusa, and she is our only survivor."

Xabthos looks at Medusa and the statues, asking, "Where is the beast that killed them?"

"There's nothing else here," said Pythios with suspicion.

Medusa unintentionally looked away, but then Perseus said, "Medusa believes the serpent swam away."

Swam away?" scoffed Xabthos. "You expect us to believe that bullshit?"

Perseus replied, "She was at the temple praying when the attack happened."

51

"Out praying! Perseus, you are so naive," said Pythios, taking another step toward Medusa.

Xabthos said, "She must be a witch! She probably cast some magical spell on her people to take control of the island."

"I agree," said Pythios.

Perseus countered, "And what grounds do you have to prove that? They were her priesthood."

Pythios said, "You can't be certain with witches also. She no longer serves any purpose."

"Guys, let's not jump to conclusions," Perseus interjected, positioning himself protectively in front of Medusa. "We can't just assume every woman we encounter is the serpent."

"Perseus, move aside! Our father won't be pleased if we return empty-handed," Pythios insisted. "We need a serpent, or else we'll have to settle for a witch."

"But we can't risk killing an innocent priestess," Perseus countered, standing his ground.

"You clearly don't understand our father," Pythios retorted.

Pythios threatened, raising his blade and advancing toward Perseus and Medusa. "He suggested using you as bait. Maybe he won't be disappointed if you don't return," he said. "If you don't let us take the girl, then we'll have a problem with you."

"But if you both claim her head, who will be crowned king?" Perseus interjected, a hint of amusement in his voice.

"Me!" they both exclaimed simultaneously, their rivalry apparent. Perseus chuckled. "Seems like you two have some issues to sort out amongst yourselves." Before anything escalated further, Xabthos declared, "Father will choose me. I'm the eldest and his favorite." Pythios couldn't contain his anger and swung a fist at Xabthos, igniting a fight between the brothers.

"Great," Medusa muttered sarcastically, realizing the chaotic situation. Perseus turned to Medusa and advised, "You should probably find a place to hide." "Agreed," she replied, swiftly making her way to the docks—the one location where she might find some genuine safety."

***

"This is the most fun I've had in years!" exclaimed Arachne.

"I'm glad you're enjoying yourself," replied Medusa, gasping for breath as she sprinted for her life.

She swiftly untied the first boat, pushing it out, and leaped on board. Perseus chased after her, shouting from the dock, "I told you to hide, not take my boat."

In response, Medusa stated, "Your brothers will find me no matter how hard I hide. It's a small island."

Grinning mischievously, Perseus raised an eyebrow and inquired, "Do you know how to sail then?"

"I will figure it out," Medusa determinedly declared.

"Well, not on my boat," declared Perseus as he jumped into the water. Within moments, he located the cold, hard steel of his sword. Pulling himself back on board, he pointed his blade toward Medusa.

"What makes you think you can take my boat? I just helped you escape those bloodthirsty idiots."

"Sorry, I just wasn't a big fan of your family," Medusa retorted. "Well, that makes two of us, but it doesn't mean you can take my boat."

"I need to find the serpent and avenge my people."

"Well, that makes two of us. I've also vowed to kill this serpent and reclaim my throne."

Perseus laughed sarcastically, his earlier skepticism giving way to begrudging respect. "Fine, then you can come." Perseus sarcastically remarked, "How generous of you to let me sail my ship," lowering his blade.

The ship left port with the calm sea and bright sun overhead.

However, their hopes for a smooth journey were soon shattered, the sky darkened within minutes, and an eerie fog rolled in. The last sight that greeted Medusa was Pythios and Xabthos yelling cries of "traitor!" and "witch!" from the dock as they sailed into the fog.

Chapter

Eleven

As nightfall descended upon them, Perseus lit candles and huddled near Medusa.

Perseus asked, breaking the tension, "We still haven't decided how to find this sea serpent."

Still exhausted, Medusa replied, "I'm not sure."

Sarcastically, Perseus suggested, "Well, we can just sail around, hoping it will attack our ship."

Chuckling softly, Medusa responded, "Maybe. Or we can simply go as far from your brothers as possible."

Agreeing with a smile, Perseus leaned into Medusa. "Yes! I like that! Let's go as far away from my horrible brothers as possible."

Drawing closer to Medusa, he placed his hand on Medusa's shoulder, and they gazed at each other, leaning in together as if drawn by a magnetic force.

Suddenly, Perseus pulled back and exclaimed, "There's a spider on you! Don't worry. I'll kill it." He reached out to grab Arachne from her veil.

Terrified, Arachne screamed, "No!" She jumped off and ran away. Perseus pulled away in confusion. "I swear that spider spoke to me!" Pretending she hadn't heard, Medusa asked, "Is it gone?"

"Sorry, I missed it, but it left. It's been a long day," Perseus remarked, sipping his wine.

"It's been rather uneventful, hey," Medusa replied, sipping her wine. However, as she drank, her eyelids grew heavy.

Perseus smiled warmly and suggested, "Would you like to go to sleep? You should get some rest."

Medusa tried to shake off her weariness and replied, "I don't think I'll be able to sleep. I haven't been able to rest properly since the attack."

"You should try, though," Perseus countered.

Despite having just survived an attempt on her life and lost everyone she had ever known, Medusa couldn't deny that Perseus's actions were adorable. Undeterred, he led her into the cabin and placed her in bed. Instantly, Medusa felt safe, falling into a much-needed sleep.

**

The Serpent grew to a height of 12 feet. That evening, Athena went to the glass fountain, trying to escape from it. However, the serpent emerged, glowing, and spoke to her. It hissed bitterly, "The more you grip the flames of envy's snare, the more you'll suffer, consumed by despair."

Athena understood the meaning behind the words but couldn't grasp how they would be of assistance. Instead, the water in the fountain grew murky and began rushing faster down the streets, causing Athena's shoes to become soaked as she waded through it.

Frustrated, she yelled at the Serpent. "Look at what you've done!" You only make things worse! She left the fountain, contaminating the drinking water. She desperately needed a new source of clean water, but the summer drought and the accompanying wildfires had exhausted her. More problems faced her than solutions.

Chapter

Twelve

As the morning light gently bathed the room, Medusa stirred, finding Perseus asleep. Her gaze fixated on him, captivated by the radiant golden glow from his skin and lips. Excitement surged within her as she imagined running her fingers along his skin and tenderly caressing his lips.

However, a twinge of fear tugged at her heart, reminding her of the potential consequences that hovered over her actions. Her serpents hissed in warning as she extended her hand toward Perseus. "He'll never love you," they cautioned, their voices filled with doubt and caution.

"Hush," Medusa whispered back, resolute in her determination to embrace this fleeting moment of intimacy with the man she had grown to love. She refused to let fear dictate her choices. "I won't allow fear to control me," she declared, her heartbeat echoing with anticipation and unease.

With a defiant and determined spirit, she reached out and delicately brushed her fingertips against Perseus's cheek, relishing in the warmth of his skin and the tender softness of his lips. In that fleeting touch, she found solace, momentarily defying the warnings and embracing the courage to pursue her desires.

Later, when Perseus awoke, he discovered Medusa preparing breakfast on the dock. They indulged in a delightful meal of fresh bread and wild fruit while the sun rose, casting a mesmerizing pink and orange glow over the water. It was the beginning of a beautiful day.

After breakfast, they secured the boat and strolled along the beach, enjoying each other's company.

The sand caressed their feet with its warm and soft touch as they paused to witness the crashing waves against the shore. A profound tranquillity enveloped them in that fleeting moment, weaving an atmosphere of profound peace and connection.

The two Greek figures revelled in the warmth. Medusa leaned against a tree, basking in the sun's gentle caress on her face, her eyes closed. Perseus sat cross-legged, hands clasped, deep in contemplation as he gazed at her. He pondered whether he would ever find his way back home and whether that was a desire he harboured.

Medusa broke the silence, speaking softly. "I'm curious. What happened to your mother?" she inquired.

Perseus sighed before beginning his complex tale. "It all started when an Oracle warned my grandfather, King Acrisius, that his daughter Danaë's son would be his downfall. In response, he confined her in a bronze chamber exposed to the sky, aiming to prevent this prophecy. However, the gods, moved by pity, impregnated her with a golden rain."

Gathering his thoughts, Perseus continued, his voice carrying the weight of the past. "My grandfather discovered the truth and grew furious. But before he could take action, he was struck by lightning and perished. For a few years, life seemed relatively normal for my mother as she was coerced into marriage. But then, she mysteriously vanished."

Medusa's eyes widened in surprise. "Do you know what happened to her?" she asked, her voice filled with concern.

"After years of uncertainty, I caught wind of rumours. It is said that she was encased in a steel chest and cast away into the sea," Perseus revealed, his words heavy with emotion.

"That's utterly terrible," gasped Medusa, her heart filled with sympathy.

"My Strategos believed it was my stepfather's doing to gain full control over Athens. He even claimed that I was meant to accompany her," Perseus disclosed.

"That's truly horrific," Medusa commiserated.

"Sometimes I wish I had." Muttered Perseus

You should not carry the burden of guilt, for you are not responsible for the actions of others.

"No I wish I had, because then I could have helped her" Perseus said remorsefully.

"Don't say that," Medusa replied, trying to console him.

"I mean it. I could have helped her," Perseus explained.

"But you were just a child. Did you ever ask her who your father is?" Medusa inquired.

"Yes, but I was so young. Sometimes I think I might have dreamt it," Perseus admitted.

"What did she say?" Medusa asked, intrigued.

"You're going to think I'm mad," Perseus warned.

"Oh, I doubt that. I've heard some wild stories before," Medusa encouraged him.

"She said it's Zeus," Perseus revealed.

"Really?" Medusa gasped, realizing that would make him a demigod.

"Yes, but I've never felt like one," Perseus confessed.

"Zeus doesn't answer your prayers?" Medusa asked, curious.

"No. He's probably too busy with his other illegitimate children," Perseus says sarcastically.

"The gods make no sense," Medusa agrees with a smile. As they sit under a tree eating fruit, Perseus asks, "So, why do you wear the veil?"" It's a sacred tradition," Medusa replies, bracing for the inevitable question. Perseus can't help but stare at the intricate headdress Medusa wears. "So you can't take it off?" he asks, his curiosity improving.

"Elders are required to wear one. It signifies our devotion and loyalty to the goddess," Medusa explains, feeling a bit self-conscious about the headpiece.

" You're an elder?" Perseus asks, surprised.

"Yup," Medusa confirms with a wry smile.

"Aren't you a little young for that?" he probes, looking confused.

Medusa shrugs. "There were limited options," she explains, then feels a pang of unease. She knows what's coming, but before her least favourite serpent whispers in her ear, "LIAR." She starts to sing to drown out the noise, masking the serpent's truthful words. Perseus begins to join her, and they spend the rest of the evening singing together. They board the boat, and Perseus shows her how to sail. They laugh and enjoy each other's company as they glide across the water. Medusa feels truly happy to be alive for the first time since the curse.

After spending hours outside, they return to the cabin. Medusa suddenly feels nervous as Perseus holds her hand, but she retracts it and says, "I'm sorry. Athena's law forbids me to touch a man."

"Athena sounds like a control freak," Perseus comments, looking slightly disappointed.

"You have no idea," Medusa agrees, relieved that he understands. "I'm not sure I'd want any idea of what it's like to be so controlled," Perseus says thoughtfully.

" And you're not controlled by your stepfather?" Medusa asks, curious. Perseus has nothing to say to that. She has made a fair point and won this argument. "You're a sharp one," he says, unwilling to verbally battle her.

***

In the middle of the night, Medusa awakens to find Perseus still asleep. Gazing at the stars, she lights a few candles, and a daring idea takes hold of her mind. Feeling daring, she pauses and whispers her prayer, "Hades, I call upon you. I will do anything to end this curse."

Then the serpents whisper, "You're a fool."

Medusa continues praying, ignoring the serpents' warning, "Please, Hades, I beg of you. Release me from this curse to free the ones I love and finally have long-lasting love."

 Another gust of wind blows out her candle, leaving Medusa feeling unsettled. She returns to bed, hoping that Hades has heard her plea.

When she wakes up, Perseus is gone. The sun has risen, and Medusa recalls her prayer to Hades, sending panic coursing through her. She rushes out of the cabin, desperately searching for Perseus.

Unable to find him, she looks high and low all over the boat. She then calls louder and louder still.

"Perseus? Perseus? Perseus!" Medusa panics, and then she hears him laugh.

"Where are you?" she yells.

"I'm right here, just swimming. Calm down," says Perseus, drifting from under the boat.

"I was just worried," says Medusa. "That's all."

"I get it; you're on edge. Unwrap and come in; relax for a while."

" I can't relax. I just lost my priesthood. Plus, aren't you worried about the sea serpent?" asks Medusa. "I'm good." Perseus lifts his tiny dagger. Medusa rolls her eyes. "I don't think that will help you against a gargantuan creature from the deep."

"Why don't you come in and protect me then, "Perseus taunts as he swims to the boat's side.

A massive wave crashes into the boat, knocking Medusa off balance. Perseus gives her a tiny pull, and Medusa plunges face first into the ocean. Panic surges through Medusa as she swims towards the surface.

Struggling to stay afloat, Medusa fights to keep her veil secure. Her soaked garments weigh her down, making it challenging to remain buoyant while clutching her veil. The thought of witnessing Perseus turning to stone and sinking to the ocean floor is unthinkable, even if it means risking her own life by drowning.

Desperate, she spots Perseus approaching and reaches out to him. He quickly seizes her and hoists her back onto the deck. Coughing up water, Medusa gasps, "I told you no!" The fear of almost causing harm to Perseus still trembles within her.

" I'm sorry. I didn't realize you were uncomfortable in the water," Perseus tries to apologize.

"I can swim," Medusa defensively snaps back.

"Swimming doesn't involve holding onto your head. Are you all right?"

"I was worried about… my outfit! It's utterly absurd that you would subject me to such a situation. What are you — a child?" Medusa's stress colors her words.

"Most people prioritize their lives over their attire, but to each their own. Who is the child here?" Perseus retorts, feeling insulted.

The palpable tension between them leaves Medusa perplexed, unable to fully grasp her own reaction. She stands up and withdraws into the cabin, leaving Perseus outside.

Once the door is shut, Arachne remarks, "You should seriously think about turning him to stone for that remark," with a touch of sarcasm in her voice.

Medusa merely smiles and retorts, "Definitely," with a sarcastic tone.

After a few minutes, Perseus knocks on the door and asks, "May I come in?"

"If you must," replies Medusa, still feeling a bit annoyed. "I shouldn't have pulled you in. I thought it would be funny, but it wasn't, and I'm sorry. I would feel terrible if the saltwater damaged your outfit," Perseus says apologetically.

"Why does it matter to you?" Medusa asks, intrigued.

" Because I love how it looks on you," Perseus says, blushing a little. "As I've said, such antics are not appropriate for mature individuals, but perhaps I overreacted," Medusa replies, smiling softly.

"Please forgive me. I would hate for this to damage how you feel toward me," Perseus says, looking genuinely sorry.

"I accept your apology and apologize for my harsh reaction. Let's move on," Medusa says, smiling back at him. Perseus smiles back, feeling relieved.

***

Athena watches with a heavy heart as Perseus's sincere apology moves Medusa. The serpent grows again, reaching nearly 14 feet. Athena had no idea what to make of this.

However, her orb reveals Poseidon, who is suddenly in Crete. Although uncertain of his plans, Athena believes his presence suggests impending trouble. She turns her gaze to see Poseidon studying Elder Sophia's statue. He walks to the water's edge and, raising his trident, commands,

"Kill the boy and bring me the girl." The ocean comes alive as an ancient beast awakens.

A nagging feeling tells Athena she bears some responsibility and should have acted sooner to prevent this. She can't help but direct her guilt towards the ever-growing serpent. After all, it was its fault.

Perseus and Medusa stumble out of the cabin as a violent tremor shakes their boat. When they step onto the deck, they stare in terror at the enormous sea serpent rising from the ocean, its massive head towering above the waves. Its dinner plate-sized eyes fix on Medusa hungrily.

Before either can react, the serpent lunges, jaws snapping dangerously close to Medusa's veil. Medusa dodges just in time, but the creature's razor-sharp, venomous teeth catch her sleeve.

The serpent hoists Medusa into the air, but she locks eyes with it and commands, "Stop this at once!"

To their shock, the serpent obeys and releases Medusa. Without hesitation, Perseus leaps forward, and with one swift motion of his sword, decapitates the beast.

As Medusa catches her breath, the serpent's body thrashes. Instead of dying, it sprouts three new heads where one once was. These new heads hiss and flash venomous teeth, preparing to strike.

In a blur of movement, one head bites deep into Perseus's shoulder, knocking him back and sending his sword skittering across the deck. As Perseus breaks free from the fangs, another head bites down on his arm and pulls him off the edge of the boat.

Medusa cries out "stop!" but the serpent ignores her plea.

With a surge of resolve, Medusa grabs Perseus's sword and throws it, piercing one of the serpent's heads. The creature bellows in pain, but the other head continues its attack, now targeting Medusa.

As the final head targets Perseus, Medusa's heart races in terror. Just then, a thunderclap resounds from the clouded skies, amplifying the scene's chaos.

Chapter
Thirteen

Pythios and Xabthos, both convinced that Medusa was a witch, set sail after her and Perseus, but their journey was soon interrupted by an ethereal and enchanting voice.

Anchoring their boats, they disembarked and followed the captivating sound until they came across a beautiful woman playing the harp and singing. The woman wore a sheer gown and continued to play as the tide washed over her feet, and the men stared in wonder. Never before had they witnessed such a thing!

After finishing her song, she asked, "To whom do I owe the pleasure of your company?"

"We are Pythios and Xabthos, princes of Athens. We are on a quest to kill a witch named Medusa," they replied.

"You must be brave or incredibly foolish to try and kill a witch."

"We are incredible brave warriors. You may provide us with dinner by wishing us good luck."

"Of course. It would be my honor."

The woman, none other than Circe, a formidable Greek witch, escorts them through the forest to her splendid marble palace. After seating them, she has Pigs serve them drinks on trays. Lifting her glass, she proposes, "To bravery, princes." As they sip, Circe subtly reveals her wand and starts a melodic tune.

"Drink, my princes,

"Drink, my pigs.

"Drink, my pig princes.

"Drink, drink, drink."

Drinking deeply, Pythios and Xabthos feel a sudden unease. Illness washes over them, and before they can voice their concerns or escape, they begin to morph. Their fingers twist into hooves, and their horrified shouts shift to panicked squeals. Clothes litter the floor, and two naked frightened pigs scamper about.

Circe, greatly entertained, watches the transformed princes. Laughing, she remarks, "Ah, delightful little piggies! You're far more charming this way. Trust me, you'll come to enjoy your new lives."

Unbeknownst to Pythios and Xabthos, they had landed on Circe's island. She had turned them into pigs, a price for their intrusion. Their days would now revolve around serving Circe, far removed from their former human pleasures.

Chapter

Fourteen

Perseus emerges from the water, victorious and shirtless. A bolt of lightning crackles in his fist, and with fierce determination, he hurls it at the serpent. The lightning strikes its target, making the beast release him and goes limp.

Medusa then yells, "Leave us!" and the serpent retreats into the ocean's depths.

Relief washes over Perseus and Medusa as they watch the serpent's departure, but then Medusa notices Perseus bleeding profusely. She assists him back onto the boat, seeing the serpent's fangs have punctured straight through his arm.

"We make an excellent team!" Perseus exclaims, a triumphant smile trying to hide his pain.

Medusa considers her response. "I suppose you truly are the son of Zeus," she acknowledges. Agony flashes across Perseus's face.

"Let me help you. We need to clean that." First, she pours salt water over the wound. After rinsing it several times, she uses a cloth to dab it and wrap it.

Guilt weighs on Medusa. Perseus lies there, drifting in and out of consciousness. Transformed into a monster, her priesthood gone. But the undeniable pull she feels toward Perseus lingers. He is the first man to show her any kindness. Hoping to relieve her guilt, she blurts out almost involuntarily.

"This is all my fault," she says.

Perseus weakly replies, "No it is not."

"I angered them, brought their wrath upon us," Medusa says as Perseus's color fades.

"I prayed to Poseidon for food," she admits.

"huh?" Perseus manages to say. "You prayed?"

Ashamed, Medusa responds, "I also turned down his proposal."

"Have you lost your mind?" he says, a bit stronger.

Medusa looks away, sheepish. "I didn't know he was divine then. Athena stepped in, seeking revenge for what she saw as my betrayal. She cursed me, and her serpent bit me. I woke up thinking I was fine until I saw my priesthood. By then, it was too late. My hair had turned them all to stone as punishment."

Perseus gazes at her and a tear slips down. He murmurs, "It's not your fault. It's the gods."

Tears stream down Medusa's cheeks as she leans forward to kiss Perseus's forehead. Her tears land on his pale skin, making him glow and heal.

Perseus sits up and smiles. "Well, that was unexpected!" He examines his now perfect arm.

They both laugh, embracing, and Perseus says, "Maybe your curse isn't so bad after all."

Medusa looks at him, she exclaims, "Yes, because there is a way to break the curse!"

"Really?" Perseus asks, surprised.

"Yes, indeed," replies Arachne, who has suddenly appeared on Medusa's veil.

"So, the spider can talk!" Perseus exclaims.

"The name is Arachne. It's nice to meet you."

"It's nice to meet you too; sorry about yesterday," replies Perseus, his voice breathy and his face deep pink. It's extraordinary to address an arachnid, but if it's speaking to him, he must follow all the ordinary rules of politeness.

"It's all good. The gods sent me to help Medusa break the curse," says Arachne.

"Break the curse?"

"They told Arachne Hades is the only god able to end Athena's curse on my people."

"Hades? Really? As in the God of the Dead?" asks Perseus. "Yes." "Then I'm afraid you are quite mad," says Perseus, looking at Medusa. "I have to try," Medusa says. "You don't understand."

"I understand you."

"You do?"

"I would have done the same for my mother, but you must be responsible. You can't possibly think you can go to the underworld and come back alive." Perseus warned.

"Then I will die trying," Medusa declared with determination.

"Fair enough, but without my help, you probably won't get far." "Without your help? You're not seriously considering joining me on this suicide mission?"

"My father sent me to kill the beast that has slain your people. Given that it is the work of the gods, I believe bringing them back is a more diplomatic solution. So, in short, I am proposing to join you." Medusa can't believe his words.

She then says, "You mean…" It's a question without a question mark, as she can't entirely assemble her thoughts. Whichever way she looks at this unholy mess.

"Yes, I wish to help you save your priesthood and way of life," he says softly, taking her hand.

" Thank you."

Perseus' father had tasked Perseus and his other sons with killing Medusa. However, she felt a sense of safety in his presence for some reason, yet carried a heavy burden of guilt for not revealing the complete truth. She knew that if he discovered she possessed serpents for hair, he would most likely kill or abandon her.

As Perseus and Medusa approach an island, they see smoke rising from afar. Hoping to find supplies to repair their boat, they row closer to shore, where the island is lush and verdant, palm trees and brightly coloured flowers framing a marble home's grand entrance.

As they near, the doors swing open, and a woman with long dark hair and golden eyes steps out to greet them. She boasts a curvaceous figure, wearing a deep blue sheer robe that cascades around her form.

"I'm Circe. Welcome to my island. For what reason have you blessed me with your company?"

"I'm Medusa, High Priestess of Athena, and this is Perseus, Prince of Athens. Our boat is damaged, and we need to carry out repairs."

"I see. What attacked it?" "I don't know what to call it," says Perseus.

"Try," says Circe coldly. "Some kind of massive sea serpent," replies Perseus. "Sounds like you've fallen into bad faith with the god of the sea."

"Yes, it appears so," Perseus answers, glancing at Medusa.

"You must be brave or incredibly foolish to consider still traveling by sea. "Definitely incredibly foolish," says Perseus.

Circe laughs. "Would you like to come in for supper? It's almost ready. There is always enough to go around, and I should appreciate the company. You have humor."

Well, Perseus was not trying to be funny, but if his so-called 'humor 'wins him and Medusa a dinner, it would be rude to decline, wouldn't it?

Medusa and Perseus look at each other and immediately reply, "We'd love to."

Perseus and Medusa stroll through the lush, tropical hallway, encountering a spectacular display of opulence. Plush carpets cover the floor, while vibrant tapestries, showcasing exotic animals in their natural habitats, decorate the walls. The vibrant colours and intricate details captivate the pair. After wandering for a few minutes, they reach the dining hall, alive with energy. Various creatures, from colourful parrots to sleek jungle cats, feast on tropical fruits and exotic meats. Luxurious tapestries, each showcasing a unique creature from the nearby jungle, hang from the walls, enhancing the wild and vibrant ambiance. Perseus and Medusa stare in disbelief at an elephant in the courtyard.

"Is that an elephant?" "Most certainly. He behaves so well." "That's incredible."

Both feel as though they've entered a magical, animal-filled wonderland.

Circe guides the trio to a lavish dining table set with an enticing array of exotic fruits and warm, freshly baked bread. A roaring fire's glow and comforting scent create a cozy atmosphere. Two pigs then present trays bearing three drinks. Circe takes the glasses and hands them to Perseus and Medusa, exclaiming, "Wonderful! Let's toast to the eve of the lunar Eclipse!" Joy shines in her eyes as she smiles at the group.

However, at the mention of "Eclipse," Medusa's heart drops. "Wait, is the Lunar Eclipse tomorrow?" she asks anxiously. Circe's face softens, and with a comforting hand on Medusa's shoulder, she clarifies that this rare event happens only once every 25 years, marking a time of wonder, not worry. Though surprised, Medusa can't shake off the feeling that big changes loom. Sensing her apprehension, Circe leans in and murmurs, "We'll face whatever comes, together," infusing her voice with determination.

They lift their glasses in a toast, but as they sip, Perseus collapses, deteriorating rapidly. Circe snatches up her wand and begins a rhythmic chant:

"Drink, my prince,

Drink, my pig. Drink,

my pig prince...

Drink. Drink, drink, drink."

As Perseus shrinks to a diminutive size, Medusa looks on in horror, shouting for Circe to halt her actions.

Chapter

Fifteen

Medusa stands horrified as a pig emerges from the clothing that Perseus had left behind. She turns to Circe, who only shrugs and says, "What a pity."

"What's in that drink? You poisoned him!" Medusa's voice trembled with anger and concern.

Circe responded with a forced smile, but her eyes revealed a mischievous glint. "I apologize, my dear. I've never been much of a mixologist. I must have mixed up the recipe. I had hoped for a dog." But the smirk on her face suggests otherwise.

"The recipe?" Medusa stammers.

Circe nods, "Yes, the recipe. Don't worry; a pig is appropriate for a prince who thinks he's above everyone else."

Medusa can hardly believe what she's hearing. "No, it's not!"

Circe shrugs, "Honestly, you're lucky you didn't end up as a little piggy yourself."

"What do you mean?" Medusa asks.

"It means that I also dislike Athena and her followers, but at least you're a woman," Circe says as she walks away.

"For the record, I hate her too," Medusa calls after her. "She cursed me already, you see. That's why I'm worried about the Lunar Eclipse."

"Princes are just as bad. Athena is full of jealousy and greed, and so are they."

"But Perseus isn't like that at all. He's kind, caring, and compassionate. He shouldn't be turn into a pig," Medusa protests, looking at Perseus the pig.

"And what about your curse? What did Athena do to you?" "She turned my hair into serpents, and then I accidentally turned everyone I love to stone!" Medusa says blatantly.

"It could be worse. You could be stranded on an island forever, like me," Circe says with a sigh.

"It could be worse? I lost my whole family, my hair was turned to serpents, and you just turned the guy I like into a pig," Medusa points out.

"He's just a man. They never do anything out of kindness. Trust me, I know," Circe says.

"Even if that's true, he's still been kind to me," Medusa argues.

"You're just blinded by hormones," Circe retorts before she walks away.

"No, his brothers wanted to kill me. He betrayed them to help me and even defeated a sea serpent that I believe Poseidon sent to assassinate me. And now, he was willing to risk his life again for me before…."

"Before he turned into a pig," Circe interrupts, shrugging. "But I must admit, it does paint him in a more favorable light."

"Please, change him back," Medusa pleads.

"Fine, I will change him back. But on one condition," Circe declares.

"What is your condition?" Medusa inquires.

"Show me your serpents," Circe requests. "It's a small sacrifice."

"But they could harm you," Medusa cautions, concern evident in her voice.

"My dear, I have been searching for something to end my existence for centuries. I highly doubt they can pose a threat," Circe smirks.

"Perseus must not see," exclaims Medusa.

"Leave that to me," assures Circe. With a flick of her wrist, Perseus, the pig, is swiftly thrown into the broom closet, and the door is slammed shut.

Medusa then slowly removes her veil, revealing her serpents. The serpents coil around her head, feeling exposed and vulnerable as they hiss. "Turn him back now," they warn, their threatening tone unsettling to Medusa.

"There you go, now you have seen them," Medusa says, trembling.

"They're stunning," comments Circe, admiration lacing her words as she looked at Medusa's serpents. "Can I cover them again?" asks Medusa, her hand instinctively reaching up to protect and silence her serpents.

Circe nods. Medusa carefully replaces her veil, ensuring it tucks securely underneath. Circe walks to her cabinet, releases Perseus, then fetches a potion. She forces the potion down the pig's throat, taps him three times on the head with her wand, and moments later, he transforms back into a human. However, he is now naked.

Medusa is relieved, and Perseus doesn't seem to mind that he is naked as he hugs and thanks her. Medusa then thanks Circe as well. "Now, I guess you'll be off to the underworld?" Circe asks. "Yes, do you know the way?" Medusa asks. "I have a gateway on my island," Circe says. "Normally, it's not a great option, but I think it'll work for you three."

Medusa and Perseus exchange hopeful glances. "Anything that can take us to the underworld is worth trying," Perseus says.

"Thank you for your help, Circe," Medusa adds gratefully.

Chapter

Sixteen

In her temple, Athena stands, fixing her eyes on Medusa, filled with a mix of anger and frustration. She believes Medusa's very existence tarnishes her reputation as a goddess. Surely, all the other gods revel in Medusa's plot for revenge.

Suddenly, Poseidon enters the temple. Athena scowls at him, her irritation deepening.

"You seem to let this one girl occupy many of your thoughts," Poseidon says with a sly grin, taunting Athena.

"She means nothing to me," Athena snaps back. The serpent's head grows larger, circling Athena in protection.

"Oh, really?" Poseidon taunts further. "Did your powerful curse come from your emotions towards me or her?" He appears unfazed by the serpent.

"Enough!" Athena shouts, her frustration growing as the serpent hisses.

"Maybe it's not her fault," Poseidon persists. "My infatuation with her could be clouding your judgment."

"I said enough!" Athena yells, her disdain for him palpable. "Leave my temple. I do not tolerate your presence here."

With that, Poseidon vanishes, leaving Athena seething in anger and frustration.

***

Circe, Arachne, Perseus, and Medusa press forward, pushing through the dense jungle until they finally reach a small, ominous black door. Flickering green flames on either side of the entrance create a sense of foreboding. Circe gestures toward the door and proclaims, "This is the entrance."

"Thank you for leading us here," Medusa expresses her gratitude. Circe settles herself on a rocky ledge and begins to speak, "Only those betrayed by the gods can pass through this door. All others will be denied entry." Medusa looks skeptically at the door and asks, "How do you know this?"

"I have witnessed countless attempts to open this door, all unsuccessful," Circe replies. "But those forsaken by the gods may pass."

Mulling over Circe's words, Medusa nods in comprehension. Stepping forward, she focuses on her deep connection with Athena through the serpents coiling around her head, and she whispers her intentions, "I will not let you separate me from those I hold dear."

A moment of silence envelops the air, but then the door begins to creak open slowly, emitting an eerie green glow. Revealing a daunting staircase that descends into the depths of the underworld. Perseus extends his hand to Medusa. "Now, let us embark on this journey to Hades and bring this to an end," he proposes, his expression resolute.

Together, they walk down the stairs and find a sleeping three-headed dog.

"That is Cerberus. How will we get past it?" Perseus whispers.

A voice from Medusa's veil says, "Maybe if we stay quiet, it will let us pass." Arachne comes out from her hiding spot.

After a few tense moments, they tiptoe around the round room. Sighing with relief, Perseus and Medusa quietly pass the sleeping guardian.

Two identical doors stand before them.

Perseus tries the first door, but it locks him out. The second door also resists his efforts. Frustration grows as they search for a way forward. Arachne jumps off Medusa's veil to tackle the first lock.

"How do we determine the right door?" Perseus questions.

Closing her eyes and taking a deep breath, Medusa says, "I believe we'll just know."

The first door opens to reveal mere rock. They hurry to the next door, keeping an eye on the slumbering Cerberus. Arachne starts working on the next lock, but then she suddenly cries out in pain. Medusa and Perseus whirl around, concerned.

"Are you alright?" Medusa inquires, worry clear in her voice.

"I managed," Arachne responds, falling into Medusa's hands as the second door opens. With determination, Medusa enters, only to find a much smaller door inside a small room. Perseus then spots one of Cerberus's eyes lazily gazing back at them.

Cerberus stirs. Arachne swiftly unlocks the third, tiny door, allowing Medusa to scramble through. Perseus attempts to follow, but Cerberus hurls a blast towards the door. With his shield, Perseus deflects it.

In a rush of panic, Medusa grabs his two legs and pulls him through the small door just as the creature launches more fiery blasts. They forcefully shut the door, narrowly avoiding harm.

Worn out and shaking, Medusa, and Perseus falls onto the hard ground, on high alert.

Hope sparks in Medusa's heart as she lifts her head. An eerie sight meets her gaze: a twisted tree with a knotted trunk and heavy branches, encircled by a pit full of completely black serpents.

"How in the blazes can we obtain that?" Perseus asks, his eyes fixed on an inscription on the wall: "Suffer a bite and face eternal damnation."

The fruit emits a warm glow, casting an eerie light on the many serpents. Time presses on, and as Medusa begins her advance, Perseus stops her. "Have you gone mad?"

"To break the curse, I must," Medusa declares, her voice firm.

"But it's 20 feet up. Not to mention the serpents. How will you reach it?"

"Fire a lightning bolt at the tree. It might drop the fruit."

"And if you can't or miss?"

A softness creeps into Perseus's eyes, and he releases Medusa. She steps cautiously, saying, "Then leave it to me. We must have that pomegranate." The serpents on her head begin to move As she approaches the treacherous pit, they part for her. Their hissing carries a message: "Theee Serrrpent Quueeeen."

With courage, Medusa delves into the pit. The serpents yield to her. Positioned below the fruit, she commands, "Fire now! I'll catch it!" In his desperation to aid her, Perseus tries to fires a bolt at the branch, but nothing happens. "It's not working."

"Then it's time for plan B," Medusa states and rallies the serpents to her side. They stack up, forming a pyramid, and elevate her. Their cold, scaly forms press against her. She reaches out hesitantly and takes the fruit.

The room's energy shifts abruptly. The serpents scatter into the walls, and Medusa plummets, only to find herself in a swing Arachne made. She gasps for air, attempting to compose herself.

Shadowy forms descend rapidly from the ceiling, surrounding the group. As her hope dwindles and the serpents flee, Medusa, clutching the pomegranate, dashes from the pursuing spiders.

Perseus struggles to harness his powers against them. Their frantic escape leads them to a platform that overhangs a vast chasm. He peers into the void, then questions Arachne, "Do you have a plan to halt them?"

Arachne chuckles, "They seek more than just friendship."

Confused, Perseus inquires, "What do you imply?"

Arachne rolls her eyes, clarifying, "They're chanting, 'Dinner. Dinner. Dinner.'"

Suddenly, a bright light starts to glow, and then a massive serpent materializes in front of the cave entrance. It is the serpent that once bit her. Yet, its presence makes the spiders flee in fear.

Medusa eyes the dark green serpent suspiciously, but it turns and glides down the winding staircase.

With renewed determination, they navigate the hazardous path ahead.

They have traveled for twelve hours, exhaustion wearing them down, but it seems they have only covered half the distance. They spot a thin stream of light at the basin, which lures them in. The steps are narrow and dangerous, but Medusa, Arachne and Perseus, determined not to lose sight of the serpent, press on. Taking a moment to rest on the cold rock, they observe the light resembling a flowing river.

They descend the steps, each engrossed in their thoughts. Soon, they encounter another source of light. Thousands of bodies drift on its surface, their combined voices singing in a haunting harmony.

They proceed, the allure of the river proving difficult to resist. In time, Medusa arrives at its beginning, where the serpent halts. A massive archway stands ahead, from which souls pour out, but only darkness awaits beyond.

"Did it lead us to a dead end?" Arachne inquires.

Soon after, a boat emerges from the archway, with a slender pale man disembarking. Lord Charon, standing by his worn wooden vessel, greets them, "Welcome to the underworld. I am Lord Charon, guardian of the River Styx."

Medusa, Perseus, Arachne, and the ancient serpent stand out among the usual souls who venture to meet the God of the dead. Charon's skeletal face gives nothing away as he asks with steady composure, "What desperation drives you here?"

Gathering her courage, Medusa states, "We seek Hades."

Charon ponders for a moment, then responds, "Hades isn't fond of visitors, but I'll ferry you to him if you're set on it."

Perseus interjects, "What pleases Hades?"

Charon warns, "He reigns over the Dead. Souls, gathered and controlled, are his desire."

Medusa addresses Perseus, Arachne, and the serpent, "You've all done so much for me already. Turn back."

Arachne takes Medusa's hand, vowing, "I promised to guard you. I'm not leaving."

Perseus's voice carries both fear and unwavering resolve. "The gods wronged you as they did my mother. I failed her, but I can defend you." The surrounding silence amplifies his words, and the now smaller serpent goes onto the boat, reinforcing their collective determination.

Guilt gnaws at Medusa as the rest board the ship, prompting her to confess to him the whole truth.

Trepidation evident in her voice, Medusa begins, "Perseus, there's something you must know."

Concerned, he inquires, "What, Medusa?"

She admits, with raw vulnerability, "I am the serpent you were tasked to slay. Serpents have replaced my hair, and they petrify those who look upon them."

Perseus's gentle smile conveys understanding, not judgment. "I had my suspicions. They've hissed throughout our journey."

Bewildered, Medusa asks, "But why come with me? My plea to Poseidon led Athena to curse me. My Priesthood saw the curse first. They're gone because of me."

Medusa's heavy confession lingers between them. Compassionately, Perseus asks, "Did you wish them harm?"

"No!" she exclaims, pain evident.

"Could you have stopped it?"

She shakes her head, "No."

"You aren't to blame," Perseus asserts. "The gods are at fault, not you." And the serpent hissed in agreement.

Gratitude fills Medusa as she hugs Perseus, who then surprises her with a kiss. The gesture revitalizes her.

Arachne and the serpent, witnessing this, smile in approval.

Medusa and Perseus, lost in their world, board the ship. As they begin their journey down the river, Charon waves them off. Arachne quips, "Guess we're navigating without a guide."

The couple exchanges a glance and chuckles, united in their determination to face the looming challenges. The boat, though old and worn, with its rotting planks and frayed sails, will serve for their voyage into the underworld's depths.

Chapter

Seventeen

Hades watches Medusa in his orb, growing more interested by the moment, and finds it hard to believe Perseus's reaction to her confession. He looks for the souls of their loved ones. For Perseus, he selects his mother, for Medusa her father, and for Arachne her best friend. Bitterness consumes him as he plays his violin and sings a mournful song.

"In the darkness of the deep,

My Violin begins to weep.

It's a mournful sound, so bittersweet,

Draws mortal souls to my keep.

For I am death's king, you see,

Collecting souls with my melody.

The music sweeps through the river, and three faces slowly emerge on the water's surface. The face of Medusa's father appears before her. She can't explain why, but she remains captivated by them as they sing to her.

The image of Arachne's friend materializes in the water, first faintly, then more clearly. Arachne has always loved her but never admitted it. As she touches her friend's hand, excitement fills Arachne's heart. At that touch, a shiver shakes her, and she senses her soul drifting away. The Serpent attempts to shield their vision, but to no avail. As long as they can see, resistance is futile.

As her friend's soul shimmers in the water, Arachne's sense of self begins to wane. Though she has always cherished her friend, her emotions now overwhelm her. When she tries to speak, Hades' voice emerges. He captures her soul, and she falls under his control.

With the image of her dear friend in front of her, Arachne's haunting melody resonates through the dark waters. Her body shines more brightly with each note, but her very essence diminishes, overtaken by Hades's power. As she sings the last note, her body collapses, devoid of life. The underworld takes her soul, leaving an empty vessel. Yet, the body miraculously returns to its human shape, as if no curse ever touched it.

Realizing the urgency, the Serpent grabs a piece of wood, and it hits them, knocking both unconscious.

Upon awakening, they discover Arachne's lifeless form, as cold as if she had lain dead for hours. Raising their eyes, they see a grand castle, illuminated by a nearly total lunar eclipse.

Her heart races as she narrowly avoids the tragic fate that befell Arachne. Her father's voice echoes in her ears, and holding onto the memory, she recognizes she isn't the vulnerable orphan she used to be. Perseus holds her, kindling her inner strength, and they stop their boat journey. Medusa sets her eyes on the looming castle illuminated by ghostly moonlight.

Chapter Eighteen

Medusa, Perseus, and the Serpent stand in front of Hades' castle's tall doors. Medusa pauses, then pushes the doors open. Inside the dimly lit hall, Hades sits on his throne, grinning slyly.

"Welcome. Glad you could join us, Medusa," Hades says, his voice dripping with sarcasm.

Faceless cloaked guards grab Perseus and the Serpent. To avoid angering Hades, both offer no resistance. The guards chain Perseus and put the Serpent in a small glass chamber.

"Hello, Hades," Medusa responds cautiously, her voice filled with caution.

"I watched your journey closely. You three have god-worthy talents.

Shame your companion couldn't keep up," Hades mocks.

Taking a deep breath, Medusa states her intention. "I brought the pomegranate of the Underworld from our challenging journey."

"We embarked on this quest to save those dear to me. Yet, I lost another who became dear along the way," emotion thickens Medusa's voice.

Hades leans forward, eyes sparkling with curiosity. "Love her, do you? Show me the pomegranate."

"I couldn't have done it without her," Medusa says, pulling the pomegranate from her pocket and offering it to Hades. The Serpent reacts by slamming its head against the glass. Medusa attempts to dismiss the serpent's erratic behavior before finally giving the fruit to Hades.

Studying the fruit, Hades remarks, "The funny thing about this fruit? Gods can't pick it. Mortals must." He chuckles, "But you did well."

Medusa feels foolish for giving up the pomegranate so easily. Emotions stir, but she steadies herself. "Help me save those I love, and promise me Perseus and the Serpent are set free," she asks Hades.

His smile broadens. "I promise. But everything has its price. Will you pay?"

Fear grips Medusa as she inquires, "What price?"

Hades meets her gaze. "Die before the eclipse ends to break the curse. After, you'll turn immortal, and your curse becomes permanent."

"No, Medusa!" Perseus shouts, but guards silence him.

Time presses on Medusa. The idea of self-sacrifice looms large. "I agree, but free Perseus," she asserts.

Hades nods. "Agreed. But once you're mine, no turning back."

Medusa thinks of Arachne. "Can you spare her? She aided me. She shouldn't die by your hand," she begs.

Hades shakes his head. "No, Medusa. The Full price must be payed." Medusa's stomach churns, but she remains focused on justice for Melia and her presiesthood.

With resolve, Medusa steps forward and kneels. Hades draws his sword, and in one swift motion, cuts through Medusa's neck. Perseus's stifled cries echo, but Hades silences him with a shout, "ENOUGH!" He turns Perseus into a rat..

Chapter

Nineteen

Searing relief surges through Medusa as her head falls. She grasps the cost of her actions but remains resolute in her decision. Her sacrifice frees her priesthood from her curse. Her body returns to its former state, and she falls to the ground.

The tiny serpent now becomes Athena, and her prison shatters. Hades looks at her, unsurprised. As Medusa's soul begins fading into a shimmering river, Athena shouts. Her voice quivering, she admits, "I was wrong, Medusa." She grasps her last chance to say those words.

Athena dashes forward, attempting to grasp Medusa's fading soul, pulling her from the water. Hades, wearing a wicked grin, watches the scene. "You're too late," he boasts, savouring his victory. Tears fill Athena's eyes, and she whispers, "I know."

Hades smirks. "Who began this?" Athena meets his gaze, grasping his meaning. "You are right," she admits, her tone filled with regret. Hades tuts. "You're pathetic, but now I get what I wanted," he says, showing the pomegranate. Hades grins slyly, "She was talented. You should have valued her more." He revels in his victory.

Confused, Athena asks, "What do you want with her?"

"A servant that is loyal to only me," Hades replies, beginning to sing a blessing as he holds up the fruit. "Medusa, hear my call, Rise from death, to be my all; in the underworld, you'll be by my side, Loyal and obedient, forever to abide."

Suddenly, the river reemerges with Medusa's soul, and her head attaches to her body. She is reborn, and a black silken top barely covering her breast and a skirt reaching down to her mid-thigh appear on her. Then, a collar forms around her neck, hands, and feet, and a leash appears in Hades' hand. Her eyes sparkle with newfound radiance as her hair transforms back into serpents. Her skin takes on a velvety smoothness, and vitality courses through her, leaving her feeling more alive than ever.

"What's happening? Why am I alive? Where is Perseus? Where is the Serpent?" Medusa asks as she looks around.

Hades then reaches down and grabs Perseus the rat and says, "I couldn't let you get distracted by such affairs, and that Serpent was none other than your biggest enemy." Hades steps towards Medusa while looking at Athena.

"What did you do to him? You promised he'd be set free." Medusa questions, her voice laced with disbelief.

Hades retorts, attempting to draw closer and kiss her, "He is free. I never said a free human." Hades laughed.

"Are you kidding me?" Medusa scoffs, taken aback by his audacity.

"Are you taking this seriously, or would you rather I crush your boyfriend?" Hades taunts, his grip on Perseus tightening.

"I apologize," Medusa swiftly responds, her words fueled by fear.

Hades presents the pomegranate seed to Medusa, remarking, "You must consume this seed."

Without hesitation, Medusa snatches the seed from Hades 'grasp. In distress, Athena's voice rings, "Don't eat it, Medusa! The one who feeds you the fruit of the underworld will hold control over you for eternity. You must resist."

Medusa turns towards Athena and can't help but remark, "I'm surprised you didn't try to feed it to me."

Regret fills Athena's eyes as she pleads with Medusa, "Medusa, I was wrong. I should have never cursed you."

Hades laughs and turns to Athena. "Silence! She is no longer yours to command," he exclaims.

Medusa hesitates as she looks from Hades to Athena, unsure who to trust.

"Now eat the seed," Hades threatens as Perseus bites a chunk out of Hades, and he howls in pain. He throws the rat to the floor knocking Perseus unconscious, but this gives Medusa an idea. With unease, she places the seed in her mouth, hides it under her tongue, and pretends to swallow it.

Hades, smug with satisfaction, gestures for Medusa to come forward and greet her new master. As she nears him, he leans in and whispers into her ear, urging her to seduce him. Playing her part, Medusa begins to weave a spell of allure, feigning an enchantment by Hades 'presence.

However, in a swift turn of events, her serpents sink their fangs into Hades' neck, causing him to recoil in pain. Seizing the opportunity, Medusa spits the seed deep down his throat with all her might. She watches as he chokes and writhes in discomfort, his futile attempts to expel the seed proving fruitless. In the face of his agony, Medusa stands resolute, unyielding in her defiance. He then charges towards her and says, "Your insolent wretch!" seething angrily.

Medusa dodges his attack and snaps, "Enough with your crass language!" Hades immediately falls silent.

Hades charges at Medusa again, but now says "stop moving", and he freezes in place, unable to move. Athena is amazed. "You have power over the God of the Dead," she says in wonder.

Medusa then turns her attention to her fallen friends in the boat and declares, " "Bring Arachne and our loved ones back to life! In all their former glory!" Although Hades hesitates, he says, "I have control over their souls, but I can't create new bodies."

Medusa rebuts, "Well, Arachne still has a perfectly usable body." He glares at her, realizing he has no choice but to grant her request. He lifts her soul from the river with a bitter heart, and she is immediately reborn into her body.

"Now turn Perseus back into a human," demands Medusa.

"I'm afraid gods still can't break their own curses. Surely you should know that by now," Hades chuckles. "Perhaps I can help," says Athena. And Athena turns to Perseus, transforming him back into a human. His body seems to radiate forgiveness and love.

Medusa is amazed and says, "Thank you, Athena."

Athena, in turn, is astonished by Medusa's newfound power. "You truly have a gift, Medusa," she remarks, impressed by the woman's bravery and use of strategy.

Then Hades declares, "A woman won't control me," and throws himself into the river and disappears.

"We should get going," says Medusa. "I agree," says Perseus. "I can take you back to Crete on my chariot," Athena smiles. "Let's go," Medusa says, and they all climb aboard. The chariot flies at unprecedented speeds. Moments later, they reappear in the sky. Athena flies back to Crete, and they dismount the chariot; it feels fantastic.

Medusa looks at Perseus and says, "Beyond all belief. I can't believe we made it."

Perseus smiles and says, "Nor can I." They gravitate toward each other as if controlled by magnetic forces as if the universe wants them to be together. They embrace each other tightly and kiss in a magical moment.

Medusa's ears perk up as she hears a familiar voice, causing her to look around. It's Melia! Overwhelmed with relief and happiness, she rushes towards her and embraces her tightly.

"There's someone I want you to meet," Medusa begins, but as she utters Athena's name, she realizes the goddess has vanished, and Arachne stands before them instead.

"Hey, I'm Melia," stumbles Melia, her gaze fixed on Arachne. They exchange greetings when Phaedra suddenly points an accusing finger at Medusa. "You're the freak who turned us to stone; I knew it!" she exclaims.

Before Phaedra can utter another word, however, she stumbles and falls face-first onto the ground, her feet once again petrified. Melia can't help but smile at the sight.

Suddenly, Medusa's hair begins to writhe and transform into a writhing mass of serpents. Speaking in a calm and measured tone, she approaches Phaedra. "Would you like to repeat that, or do you prefer to be able to walk?" she asks.

Phaedra trembles with fear as she stares at the terrifying sight before her, nodding frantically.

With a nod from Phaedra, Medusa regains control over her hair, reclaiming her power. Swiftly, she utilizes her abilities to unravel the curse that turned Phaedra's feet to stone, freeing her from the petrification. As they witness the reversal, Medusa's serpents hiss in approval, their voices echoing, "Good work."

Moments later, Amaltea comes into view and says, "It's nice to see you ladies getting along."

Medusa runs and embraces her in a tight embrace, grateful for their newfound unity.

Chapter

Twenty

Athena was profoundly aware of her responsibilities and clearly understood the necessary course of action. As night descended, she embarked toward the courtyard nestled at the capital's core and discovered Poseidon patiently awaiting her presence. Initially, Athena averted her gaze, but after a reflective moment, Athena mustered the bravery to turn back and acknowledge the corruption brought upon by her own greed. She confessed her recent realization that genuine wisdom and strategic acumen could only be attained by releasing trivial conflicts and prioritizing the well-being of the people she held dear. Empowered by this newfound understanding, she offered to unite forces with Poseidon, who graciously embraced her proposal.

In a surprising turn of events, Poseidon admitted that he had initiated the famine, but it had exceeded his expectations. He realized that it was time for introspection and setting things right.

Athena was deeply moved by his admission and watched in amazement as Poseidon performed an unbelievable feat. He lifted the curse from the fountain, transforming the murky waters into crystal clear ones. Athena couldn't help but feel overjoyed as he bestowed his blessings upon it, effectively ending the long and painful famine.

Perseus and Medusa tell the King that they broke the curse, but despite their valiant efforts, the King denies Perseus the throne, insisting that only his real sons deserve it. Overwhelmed by the prolonged wait, the stepfather goes mad and tries to execute Perseus on the spot. However, he doesn't realize the loyalty and support that backs Perseus. Perseus asks Medusa to turn his stepfather into stone. She grants his wish, and they place the stepfather as an ornament in their new royal garden.

Greece entered a remarkable golden age and basked in prosperity. After many years of successful governance, both Medusa and Perseus chose to step down and institute the first democratic government. They retired to Circe's island and lived happily ever after, with two remarkably well-behaved pigs tending to their every need.

Printed in Great Britain
by Amazon

27533077R00066